PUFFIN BOOKS

# THE JOKE SHOP

Ian Strachan was born in Altrincham, Cheshire, in 1938. He was educated at Altrincham County Grammar School, the Royal Academy of Dramatic Art and the Central School of Speech and Drama. He is married with a son and a daughter. Having worked as a theatre stage director, radio presenter and television producer, he is now a full-time writer of short stories, children's books and novels, many of which have also been published in USA and Japan and regularly translated into most European languages. Ian Strachan lives in the country, and enjoys foreign travel and hillwalking.

*Another book by Ian Strachan*

MOSES BEECH

# SURFERS

# The Joke Shop

Ian Strachan

Illustrated by
Ron Tiner

PUFFIN BOOKS

PUFFIN BOOKS

Published by the Penguin Group
Penguin Books Ltd, 27 Wrights Lane, London W8 5TZ, England
Penguin Books USA Inc., 375 Hudson Street, New York, New York 10014, USA
Penguin Books Australia Ltd, Ringwood, Victoria, Australia
Penguin Books Canada Ltd, 10 Alcorn Avenue, Toronto, Ontario, Canada M4V 3B2
Penguin Books (NZ) Ltd, 182–190 Wairau Road, Auckland 10, New Zealand

Penguin Books Ltd, Registered Offices: Harmondsworth, Middlesex, England

First published 1997
3 5 7 9 10 8 6 4

Filmset in Bembo

Made and printed in Great Britain by Clays Ltd, St Ives plc

A CIP catalogue record for this book is available from the British Library

ISBN 0–140–38057–4

# Contents

# SCIENTISTS BAFFLED

The discovery of a number of modern objects, including a current English coin, a brand-new pair of trainers and a maths textbook, in a remote part of the Australian desert has puzzled scientists. The objects were found by a group of Aborigines on their annual walkabout and led to a widespread police search of the area. Police, suspecting foul play, used helicopters with heat-seeking devices to scour the desolate area, but nobody, alive or dead, was found.

## English link

Scientists were brought in after it was discovered the book contained the name of an English school and that the particular make of trainers had never been sold outside the UK. Scientists are now working on the theory that the objects could somehow have dropped from a plane. But Mrs Stone, the head teacher of the English school, says, 'No pupil from this school has either holidayed in, or emigrated to Australia during the past ten years.'

## Chapter One
### *Condini's*

"Hey, Bren, look at that! Have you ever seen anything so . . ." Rory leapt up and down in excitement, ". . . so fantastic?" If he'd had wings, he'd have been flying up into the darkness.

For weeks Rory had been waiting for

this moment. Every day, on the way home from school, we'd passed the hoarding which bulged out on to the pavement. The sound of workmen banging, knocking and sawing, as they fitted out the shop, had been driving Rory wild with curiosity.

But at last, just a few weeks before Christmas, the hoarding was gone and Condini's Joke Shop was finally open.

Rory's very into jokes. Me? Sure, I get the odd laugh watching people on TV being dumped in gunk, or getting custard pies flung in their faces.

But Rory not only loves all that stuff, he always wants to be the one *doing* the dumping, or flinging, and he spends every waking minute trying to invent more elaborate ways of doing it. Last week he got put in detention for spending a whole period designing, on the back of his science book, his Magnificent Pie Flinging Machine.

Afterwards, Rory showed me the drawing of what looked like a windmill, but with the sails turned the other way round. "As each one comes round," he explained, "it hurls a pie through the air and it goes round so fast, you'd easily splosh somebody four times before they knew what was happening. Neat, or what?"

"How do the pies get on there?"

"I load them on, as each sail comes round."

"And what makes them turn?" I asked, though I had a feeling I knew the answer.

"You do," he said, just as I'd expected, "by turning the handle on the side."

That sums me up. I'm Rory's sidekick. I usually keep watch, while he's setting things up and sometimes lead people into the traps he's set for them.

Now you know why the opening of the Joke Shop was such a big deal for Rory, but I had to admit, now I'd seen it, even I was impressed.

The shop window loomed out into the darkened street like an underwater cave. Around it, the shop front had been converted into a huge cliff, like one of those indoor climbing walls, with crags and caves all over it. Sometimes puffs of bluish-green smoke came out of the caves. At others they glowed red with fire, a big pair of yellow eyes peered out through the darkness at you, or menacing trolls and hobgoblins appeared.

There were loudspeakers hidden in it too, which suddenly let out ghostly groans, the rattling of chains, gunshots and even the occasional belch, or the sort of fart a whoopee cushion makes.

But in a spotlight, up on the highest peak, way above the pavement, was perched an evil-looking vulture. Its bloodshot eyes moved slowly back and forth as it watched shoppers below. You just knew it was choosing its victim; deciding which person to swoop down on, grab with its sharp talons and rip apart with its hooked beak.

I shivered. "I think it's scary."

But Rory laughed. "Can't you take a joke? Come on, let's see what's in the window."

He raced across the road, leaving me no choice but to follow. The window was lit in a blue, ghostly kind of light, but the stuff on show was mostly pretty ordinary. Plastic dog turds, itching powder and a few expensive conjuring tricks.

Rory said, "Let's go in."

"We'll be late home."

"So what?"

When we opened the door, instead of a bell to warn the shopkeeper there were customers, we heard the ghostly hoot of an owl. But there was no sign of the shopkeeper and no other customers in the shop.

It was very dark, with just a few lights

in the display cases and there was this weird smell, as if somebody had mixed mouldy biscuits with sour milk and left it to fester.

Rory was racing round, pointing out gruesome things like skulls and severed fingers. He dragged me over into a corner to admire a life-sized skeleton, glowing green in the darkness.

"Hello, boys," a rasping voice whispered from behind me.

I nearly fell over with shock! I turned to find a small, thin man, rubbing his long, bony fingers together. Long, untidy grey hair flowed over the shoulders of his shabby, black velvet jacket. The pale skin of his face was stretched so tightly over the bones, he looked just like one of the plastic skulls in the showcase.

But what worried me most was, where had he sprung from? How could he have crept up, without either of us noticing?

His powdery lips opened over yellow teeth in a leering smile, as he bowed and hissed, "I am Condini. Welcome to my humble store. You have entered a confused world, where nothing is quite what it seems, but all things become possible."

Rory's eyes opened wider than dinner-plates. "You mean, anything's possible?"

"Oh, but of course. This is the world of illusion where the unlikely happens today and only the impossible takes a little longer."

Looking round the goods on offer, I said, "Looks like all the same old phoney stuff to me."

That was when I first noticed Condini's eyes. They were such a dark blue, they were almost purple, with huge black pupils that felt as if they could see right into my mind and read my thoughts. But worse still, the cold tingle running down my spine convinced me that his eyes had the power to freeze me into a solid block of ice.

The man's arm slid round Rory's shoulder like a snake encircling its prey. "I see your friend is not a believer in our powers. Perhaps we should convince him of their strength?"

Standing next to the old man, Rory didn't see just how serious he was and laughed. "Yes, go on. You show him!"

The way the old man came towards me I expected to be turned into a toad, at least. But all that happened was, he told me to open my mouth and pretended to pull an egg out.

Although Rory smiled, he did say, "That's a bit corny."

"Indeed," Condini admitted. "Let's see what more impressive delights we can find to appeal to a sharp mind like yours."

But as the old man led Rory away, I saw him crush the eggshell behind his back. From the bits, appeared a live, green reptile with needle-sharp teeth and smouldering red eyes.

I cried out, "Rory!"

"What?" he said crossly.

But by the time Rory turned, the

creature had already slipped to the floor and scuttled out of sight beneath a counter.

Knowing Rory would never believe me, I simply shrugged it off. "Oh, forget it."

## Chapter Two
## *Impressing Natalie*

"If you like," Rory suggested to Natalie, "I could pull something out of your nose."

"That's not very clever," she replied, with a toss of her long, straight, silver-blonde hair. "Snotty Hawkins never stops

14

pulling things out of *his*!"

"What if I produce a coin out of thin air?" Rory called out anxiously, as she turned to leave. But, in too great a hurry to perform the trick for her, the coin slipped from his fingers and rolled off down the playground. By the time he'd picked it up again, Natalie had disappeared with her friends.

Apart from practical jokes and tricks, Natalie is the only other thing Rory is interested in. Or he would be if she ever gave him the chance.

"I knew I should have got the bleeding thumb in the matchbox," Rory said with a scowl. "I bet she'd have loved that."

The previous evening we'd spent ages in Condini's Joke Shop, choosing different tricks which Rory seriously believed would finally make Natalie notice him.

"Never mind," Rory said, over the sound of the first bell, "I've still got plenty of things to try out on her."

He wasn't kidding either! He'd blown two whole weeks' pocket-money at Condini's on different bits and pieces.

But it wasn't the waste of money that worried me. Far worse was the way Rory seemed to have fallen completely under the old man's oily spell.

As Rory wandered round, like a choco-holic in a sweetshop, the old man kept buttering him up, saying things like, "What an excellent choice" and "How very perceptive of you, young man."

It wouldn't have been so bad if

Condini had just been trying to separate Rory from his money but, although I couldn't quite work out what the old man was up to, I sensed something far more sinister was going on.

Rory hadn't seemed to notice. When we finally got outside, he kept raving on and on, "Isn't that the most amazing place you've ever been in, Bren?"

I tried to tell him I didn't like it, that there was something evil about the place, but he just went ranting on about how brilliant Condini was.

And when I told him about the green reptile I'd seen coming out of the egg, Rory burst out laughing. "You're the one that needs to watch it! You've started seeing things, Bren."

Then he went back to the stuff he'd

seen. "I'd love a set of those interlinking rings, or one of those knives with a blade that goes up into the handle when you stab someone. The thing is, all Condini's stuff looks so much better than usual. Most of those knives are usually tinny things you could never believe in, but Condini told me he made his as an exact replica of an Aztec sacrificial knife."

"I can believe it," I muttered. I wondered bitterly who the old man intended sacrificing? Me probably! I hadn't been the life and soul of the party in there and Condini had kept giving me filthy looks whenever I'd tried to get Rory away from him.

"Did you realize," Rory prattled on, "Condini makes most of the special tricks himself?"

At least Natalie hadn't been taken in! But that didn't stop Rory from trying. He cornered her in the dining hall during the lunch break, took out a rigged deck of cards he'd bought and started doing fancy card tricks.

"Rory! Just leave me in peace with my salad roll!"

"Pick a card, any card," he urged, thrusting the fan of playing cards under her nose.

But Natalie wasn't looking at the cards. Her widening eyes were fixed on her roll. "Ugh!" she cried. "There's a slug in there."

The funny thing was, I thought Rory had decided not to buy the box of chocolate slugs. He must have changed his mind.

I couldn't help admiring the slick way Rory operated! The card tricks were nothing more than a blind to distract Natalie's attention while he slipped the slug into her lunch.

But it wasn't the first time he'd pulled a stunt like that on her. He'd once hidden a black, rubber rat in her school bag and she'd screamed the place down when she'd found it during history.

So Rory should have known better. This wasn't the way to sneak into Natalie's affections!

Getting a hold of herself, Natalie said, "Rory, I suppose this is your idea of a joke?"

I had to hand it to Rory. He kept his face straight and managed to look totally innocent, and slightly hurt by her accusation. "Natalie, I swear, that slug's got nothing to do with me. Honest!"

Natalie shook her head. "Honest? You don't know the meaning of the word! You'd stoop to anything just to put me off my lunch, wouldn't you? Well, if you think I'm going to let one of your joke chocolate slugs ruin my food, you're wrong. Watch me!"

Even I was taken in by the way Rory swiftly leant across, frantically trying to grab her arm and pull the roll away from her mouth. "Don't, Natalie!" he shouted.

But she managed to get away, took an enormous bite and chewed it up with enormous satisfaction. "There!" she said, triumphantly. "Satisfied? Now, will you, please, leave me alone!"

Without another word, Rory got up

and left. I followed him out of the dining hall, saying, "I thought you didn't get any chocolate slugs?"

"I didn't," Rory agreed. "Whatever was in Natalie's roll had nothing to do with me."

"But if that wasn't a *chocolate* slug . . ." I said thoughtfully.

"Exactly!" said Rory.

## Chapter Three
## *The Inner Sanctum*

"I WANT SOMETHING really different,"
Rory told Condini during our next
visit.

Although I'd tried to tell him, Rory
didn't seem to understand: nothing he
bought from the Joke Shop was ever

going to impress Natalie. We'd already spent an hour in there, while Condini showed him everything from glass balls which exploded when they were dropped, to real tricks, like a walking stick which turned into a bouquet of flowers. I was bored and even Condini was getting a bit testy. "Today, nothing seems to please the young master."

"It's got to be very special," Rory insisted.

"Might one inquire why?" Condini asked.

Before Rory had a chance to answer, I said, "He's trying to persuade Natalie to go out with him."

"Oh, I see!" Condini said with a leer. "You didn't tell me there was a young lady involved." His bony hands rubbed together, rasping like two sheets of sand-paper.

"What's through there?" Rory asked, pointing towards an archway I hadn't noticed before.

The light from the opening glowed pale green, though it was impossible to tell its source as the archway was filled by some sort of vapour. Trails of the stuff snaked across the floor towards us.

Condini hurriedly tried to block Rory's view. "Oh, you've spotted my inner sanctum. I'm afraid that's a private showroom, only intended for more advanced magicians."

"Couldn't we just see inside?"

Condini shook his head. "I think that might be unwise. Maybe later, when you're more experienced."

"I only want to look," Rory pleaded.

"Ah, but will it end there?" Condini asked, and then shook his head before answering his own question. "I suspect not. Once people have seen, they usually want to touch, and before I know where I am, they're trying things. That could be exceedingly dangerous!"

The mere mention of that word had Rory completely hooked. "In what way dangerous?"

"I'm afraid," Condini explained, "that people are always too anxious to run before they can walk."

But I suddenly twigged. All the time Condini had been sounding as if he wouldn't let Rory go in, he'd been moving slowly backwards, closer to the eerie archway. The old man's caution was a total fake, meant to make Rory more curious and guarantee he would insist on going into the back room.

"Rory!" I burst out.

He turned, mystified. "What?"

"Er . . ." My mind raced, trying to think of a good excuse. ". . . I thought I saw Natalie go past. Why don't we . . ."

"Would Natalie be the young lady you wish to impress?" Condini asked. Rory nodded. To my surprise, Condini suddenly smiled, displaying his cheesy teeth. "Go, my young friend!" he urged Rory, flapping his hands as if Rory was a hen he was shooing off. "Don't waste the opportunity!"

I could tell Rory was torn between chasing after Natalie and an overwhelming interest in the mysterious back room.

"But I'd rather see . . ."

Condini held up his hand. "I can promise you, the room will still be there another day. For now, you should seize the moment with your Natalie!" And he ushered us both out through the door.

I felt better once we were outside, but Rory was busy searching the street for any sign of Natalie. "Which way did she go?"

I pointed vaguely up the High Street. "I think it was that way."

"I can't see her."

"Maybe it was the other way then," I shrugged.

Rory's eyes narrowed. "You didn't see Natalie, did you?"

"I *thought* I did."

Then light dawned on Rory. "Bren,

you liar! You didn't see Natalie at all, you just didn't want to go in the back room. You're scared!"

"No, I am not."

"You are," Rory said, poking me in the chest.

"Am not!"

"All right then," Rory said, putting his hand on the door handle, "prove it! Come back in with me."

But when Rory pressed the handle and tried to open the door, he discovered it was locked. The shop was in total darkness and there was no sign of Condini.

Rory must hardly have slept that night because he was round at my house, to pick me up for school, by eight o'clock. We were standing on the doorstep of the Joke Shop by half-past, when Condini

29

slid back the bolts. The owl over the door sounded quite sleepy as we went in.

"Ah, my young friends," Condini greeted us with his skeleton's smile. I could swear he slept in a coffin, not a bed. "I have been considering your problem." Rory looked blank. "How to impress your lady friend," Condini said with a broad leer, which sent waves of foul breath in our faces.

Not that Rory noticed, he was too excited. "And have you come up with something?"

"Condini never fails!" the old man said proudly. "Flowers always please a lady." He unclenched his gnarled fist to reveal four tiny seeds.

Rory was not impressed. "I don't have time to grow her flowers!"

"Ah, what it is to be young and impatient!" Condini sighed. "But these are instant flowers."

As the old man picked up a glass of water, Rory groaned. "Not those dreadful dehydrated things, which come out looking like bits of scrap plastic?

"Certainly not!" Condini protested, deeply offended by the suggestion. "Watch!"

Condini dropped one of the seeds into the water. Rory and I bent down, staring at the glass as the seed twirled its way to the bottom. For a moment it just lay there.

"Nothing's happening," I growled.

Condini glared at me and hissed, "Wait!"

Then the seed split, to reveal a tiny

pink dot. The dot quickly changed into a pink petal and, within seconds, there were hundreds more petals and the glass was filled by a beautiful pink flower, like one of the pompon chrysanthemums my dad grows, only far more beautiful.

But the scent was overpowering! At first I thought it was quite nice that for once the shop didn't smell of old socks, but the scent became so sickly, it was like having your nose thrust into candyfloss!

Rory was too busy gazing at the flower to notice the smell. "That's amazing!" he sighed with admiration.

"You're too kind," Condini said, with a little bow. But you could tell he was pleased by the way he smiled to himself while dropping the remaining seeds into a little plastic bag. "I only hope your

Natalie will be impressed."

"I bet she will," Rory said enthusiastically, but then his face fell as he dug into his pockets. "Trouble is, after buying those things the other day, I haven't got much money left. Aren't these very expensive?"

But Condini refused to take the money he was being offered. "Please! Take them with my compliments."

"That's very kind of you, thanks very much." Rory was so pleased with the trick, we were almost out of the shop, when he suddenly remembered. "But what about the back room? I thought you might let us see it today."

I grabbed hold of Rory and tried to pull him towards the door. "We're going to be late for school! The second bell'll be going any minute."

And, to my enormous relief, for once the old man agreed with me. "Why don't you come back after school, when you'll have more time? Besides, then you'll be able to tell me how your Natalie reacts to our little surprise."

## Chapter Four
### *Say It with Flowers*

RORY WAS SO impatient to show Natalie his latest trick, he got into trouble halfway through assembly.

He'd been bouncing about on his chair and whispering to me all the time our Headteacher, Mrs Stone, known to us as Rolling because she's big and round, was going through the notices.

Finally, while Rolling was banging on about her plan to raise money for the school funds with a special Christmas Concert, Rory turned right round and hissed at Natalie, who was sitting three rows back, "Wait until you see what I've got for you."

Nobody who heard him could resist whispering a few rude suggestions as to what it might be, but Rory wasn't going to be put off. "It's really special!" he hissed in a loud stage-whisper.

"Rory!" Rolling bellowed at the top of her voice. "You seem to have an awful lot to say this morning. Perhaps you would like to appear in the concert?"

"No, miss."

"Oh, believe me, I'm not so easily turned down, Rory. Perhaps you'd like to discuss it with me? My office, first break."

"No, miss."

Everyone giggled, until Rolling raised her eyebrow. "I beg your pardon?"

"Sorry, miss," Rory spluttered. "I meant, I still wouldn't like to appear in the concert, but I will come to your office."

Rolling's mouth twisted into a withering smile. "How very kind of you!"

As we filed out of assembly, Rory grumbled to me, "That means I'm going to have to wait for the dinner break before I can show Natalie."

"I bet she's totally crushed!" I said, but ruined it by bursting out laughing and had to duck to avoid Rory's sharp right hook.

After first break, I was quite surprised when Rory came back from his meeting with Rolling looking quite pleased with himself. "Didn't she give you GBH of the eardrums?" I asked.

Rory preened himself like a peacock. "Of course not. Mrs Stone reckons I'm very clever."

"I knew they were putting something peculiar in the water round here!" I said sarcastically.

Rory ignored me. "As a matter of fact, she thinks I've had a brilliant idea."

"What is this idea of yours?" I asked suspiciously.

But Rory waved me aside and all he would say was, "You'll find out, eventually."

By dinner break, word had got round and everyone knew Rory was up to something. Nobody wanted to miss out and even kids who normally went home or bunked off to the chippy had stayed behind.

The dining hall, which was usually half-empty, was full to bursting. Rumours must have penetrated the staff room, because there were twice the usual number of teachers on duty. I think they were expecting some kind of punch-up!

What baffled the dinner-ladies was, nobody was queuing for food. So they were quite relieved when Rory pushed through the crowd and marched up to the counter.

"Yes, dear?" said Mrs Greenhalgh.

"We've got pizza, sausages, and today's special is shepherd's pie."

"Could I just have a jug of water please?"

Mrs Greenhalgh's mouth dropped open, doubling her usual number of chins. "Pardon, dear?"

"A jug of cold water, please. I'm very thirsty."

Mrs Greenhalgh was so surprised, she handed it over without a word.

As Rory walked over to the table where Natalie was sitting with her mates, Mr Higson stopped him. "I hope that water isn't going to end up all over somebody."

"I promise, Mr Higson," said Rory politely. I noticed that, while he was talking, Rory was busy fumbling with one hand in his pocket and I guessed he was feeling for the seeds and hiding them between his fingers.

"Remember," Mr Higson cautioned, "I'm watching you!"

With a big flourish, Rory placed the jug in the centre of Natalie's table. She was looking a bit embarrassed, but Rory took no notice.

Tilting his head back and half-closing his eyes, Rory began to weave his hands backwards and forwards above the jug.

Because I knew what was going on, I saw him drop the seeds into the water, but nobody else did. When nothing seemed to be happening, they soon got restless and there were shouts of "Come on!" and "Get on with it!"

But Rory ignored them and just kept slowly moving his hands.

Catcalls and whistles broke out. Then Snotty Hawkins shouted, "Rory's got his rabbit stuck up his sleeve."

Natalie, who hated being the centre of attention, went bright red. She got up and was about to leave, when she noticed three flowers growing up under Rory's hands. One was pink, like the one in the shop, another was pale blue and the third was green.

She watched as the flowers grew larger and larger, until finally they filled the top of the jug.

Everyone clapped and it was easy to see Natalie was impressed.

I dug Rory in the ribs with my elbow and whispered, "I think you've cracked it!"

But one of Rory's problems has always

been, he doesn't know when to stop. If he'd just left her looking at the bunch of flowers, while everyone was still admiring them, everything would have been all right. But he *had* to push his luck!

"Natalie," he said, "they're specially for you."

"Yeah," Natalie said, "thanks."

"Aren't you going to smell them?" he asked.

She gave them a quick sniff, but that wasn't good enough for Rory. He lifted the jug up so far, her nose disappeared into the delicate petals. But when she pulled back, the whole crowd screamed as they saw the huge, black, hairy spider clinging to her nose.

Rory froze.

"Get it off me!" Natalie screamed,

shutting her eyes and stamping her feet.

Someone swiped at it with a tissue and as it scuttled across the floor the crowd parted. One or two leapt on to tables but Beryl Ormerod, who was made of strong stuff, caught it under a glass and whisked it off outside.

Then everyone burst out laughing, but Natalie, convinced she'd been deliberately made the butt of Rory's joke, was very upset. "Rory, if you ever again come within a mile of me, I'll kill you with my bare hands."

And she stamped off, with Rory running after her, desperately trying again to protest his innocence.

I didn't follow him because I couldn't take my eyes off the flowers. They were wilting almost as quickly as they'd grown. I was going to grab hold of them and chuck them away, when they suddenly decomposed leaving a mess of putrid, green slime running down the jug on to the table. The slime steadily began to swell, like a blob of witch's hair mousse, until it was head-sized and still growing.

Suddenly the dining hall was filled with a hideous stench, as if someone had dropped a crate of rotten eggs. Everyone ran out clutching their noses but, although I covered my mouth and nose, I stayed.

I had seen something extraordinary: yellow maggots wriggling in the slime. They seemed to be absorbing the filthy muck through their skins, and as they did, it slowly turned them from yellow to green.

But the stuff continued to swell inside them. Several maggots were already the size of rugby balls. Their sides were stretched and shiny, and they looked as if they were about to burst any second. I turned and ran.

As I got to the door I heard several loud plops, followed by squelchy splats, as if someone had hurled a bucket of frog-spawn at the walls, and there was an unbelievable smell!

## Chapter Five
### *Chicken!*

AS WE WENT through the gates after school, leaving the shouts and taunts to die away behind us, Rory grumbled, "There wasn't a spider in the flower at the Joke Shop."

"Nor gigantic exploding maggots,"

I added gloomily.

"I still think you're making that part up, Bren!"

Because I was the only one who'd seen what happened, Rory was convinced I'd invented the explosion to make him feel even worse than he already did over his colossal failure with Natalie.

"Then how do you account for the council cleansing squad turning up this afternoon?" I demanded. "All those men in masks and white overalls, who went in to sluice the whole dining hall down?"

Rory shrugged. "They probably come every year to scrape the congealed custard off the walls. I bet we've never seen it before because they usually do it during the holidays."

"Oh yes, right!"

"But I'm going to ask Condini about that spider," Rory said firmly.

I couldn't believe what I was hearing. "You're surely not going back there, not after what happened today?"

"Of course," Rory said. "I want to know what went wrong."

"Condini is totally evil, that's what's wrong," I said. "You want to stay as far away from him as possible. If you don't, I'm certain something really bad is going to happen soon."

"Have you been gazing into one of Condini's crystal balls?" Rory scoffed.

"I wouldn't buy *anything* from him," I insisted. "After today, you never know what his stuff might do."

"But they're only tricks, you idiot. It's just that his tricks are so much better than other people's."

I shook my head. "More lethal, you mean!"

Our argument had brought us all the way down to the Joke Shop and Rory already had his hand on the door. "Are you coming in, or are you too scared?"

I really didn't want to go back inside the shop, but it didn't feel right to leave Rory there on his own and anyway, I couldn't have him going round saying I was chicken.

"Couldn't we leave it for today?" I asked, hopefully.

"You can if you like," Rory said, "but I've got to ask Condini a favour for Rolling."

"For Rolling?"

But Rory went into the shop without answering and so I trailed after him.

Condini greeted us. "Ah! My young friends! And how did you get on with your Natalie?"

Rory told him all about the entire fiasco, which had left Natalie threatening to kill him if he ever went anywhere near her again.

Condini looked genuinely upset. "Oh, dear! A spider you say? I've never had anything like that happen before. Mind you, it was very old stock. Perhaps the seeds had gone bad."

"Would that explain the maggots too?" I asked

"Maggots?" Condini laughed. "I think you are teasing me."

"He's the only one who saw the

maggots," Rory explained.

"I think," Condini said to me, with a tolerant smile, "you have been allowing your imagination to run riot."

"I *did* see them!" I protested, but they both ignored me.

"I am sorry about your young lady," Condini said to Rory. "How can I make it up to you?"

"Well, there are two things you could do."

"Two!" Condini's laugh sounded like a rusty hinge squeaking back and forth. "Isn't that a little greedy?"

"One isn't really for me, it's more for my school," Rory explained. "We're having a Christmas Concert to raise funds and I suggested to our Head, Mrs Stone, who's organizing it, that you should appear, performing some of your tricks."

Then I knew why Rory had looked so pleased with himself when he'd come out of her study.

"Oh no," Condini said, shaking his grey head. "It's very kind of you to ask, but it's many years since I last appeared in public."

But once Rory had got an idea in his head, he wasn't easily put off. "I'm sure you could still do it. I mean, it must be like riding a bike, you never lose the knack."

"I'm so out of practice," Condini said modestly.

"But there's two weeks before the concert," Rory pointed out, "plenty of time to get ready."

I cut in quickly. "Rory, you heard what

the man said. If he doesn't want to do it . . ."

"It isn't that I don't *want* to do it," Condini said slyly, "but I'd hate to let you down again, in front of all your friends."

"I'm sure you wouldn't," Rory insisted.

Condini considered the idea and then said, "I tell you what, I'll think about it and let you know next week. Now, what was the other thing you wanted?"

"This morning, you said if we came back when there was more time," Rory said cautiously, "you'd show us what was in the back room."

Again, I could have sworn there was no sign of the archway when we'd first entered the shop, but when my eyes flicked across, there it was, still glowing misty green.

"So I did!" said the old man, thoughtfully rubbing the stubble on his bony chin. "You are quite certain you really want to see in there?"

"I'm not much bothered," I mumbled.

But Rory drowned me out. "Yes, of course we do."

"Very well," Condini said, "but remember, I have warned you how dangerous it can be! You must promise me you won't touch anything without my permission. Otherwise I cannot be held responsible for the results."

"We promise!" Rory said firmly, speaking for both of us.

"Very well," Condini said with a sigh, "I just hope you know what you're doing." He bowed low and waved us towards the mysterious green opening. "Please, step into the private world of Condini!"

## Chapter Six
# *The Sorcerer's Apprentice*

ON THE OTHER side of the arch, as the mist slowly began to clear, we found ourselves in a low, narrow room with wooden shelves running down either side. They were stacked with all kinds of oddments. Some were simply stock, copies of items already on display, but others looked more sinister.

Nearest to us sat row upon row of dusty old skulls, which looked frighteningly real and not at all like the plastic ones in the shop. There were also shrivelled heads, sprouting tufts of wiry, black hair and a few broken teeth, which appeared to have been shrunk. Next to them lay grimacing, carved African masks, stacked alongside Haitian voodoo dolls.

"Is that a —?" Rory's hand went out towards a brightly painted, miniature totem-pole.

But Condini grabbed Rory's arm and pulled it back.

"Remember, no touching!"

"Sorry, I forgot. Is that a real totem-pole?"

Condini gave a wistful smile. "Everything you see in here is real and yet it is also an illusion."

"You mean this stuff isn't really here?" I asked innocently.

Condini gave me a pitying smile. "You *do* enjoy your little joke, don't you, Brendon?" I was about to nod, when he fixed me with a steely glare and added, "And one day, if you don't control it, your sense of humour could be the death of you."

Rory grinned, but I felt another shiver running down my spine, as if Condini had slipped an icicle down my back.

Condini moved Rory swiftly on towards a shelf crammed with screw-top storage jars of various sizes. Though the jars were exactly the same as the ones my granny used for pickles and relish, Condini's contained disgusting-looking things. The bits, which were floating in colourless liquid, looked as if they had been stolen from a butcher's dustbin.

"What's that?" Rory asked, pointing to a spongy, dark purple object about the size of a fist.

Condini smiled proudly. "A spleen."

"And that?" said Rory. The jar held a pinky-red object like a small, narrow tongue.

"An appendix," Condini casually replied.

I forced myself to ask, "What are they all for?"

"You never know," Condini said quietly, "when someone might need a new one."

I gulped. "You mean they belonged to humans?"

"Of course," Condini snapped, adding coldly, "mostly taken from people who had a misplaced sense of humour."

Thinking Condini was joking, Rory laughed as he asked, "How do you know they had a sense of humour?"

"I can only tell you," Condini said confidentially, "that they were laughing right up to the moment I removed their organs!"

Rory's smile froze and his voice quavered slightly. "You *are* joking? Right?"

Condini gave Rory a very odd smile before he finally reassured him. "Yes, of course. Some of the newer conjurors," he explained smoothly, "enjoy shocking their audiences in rather obvious ways. Rather than producing a rabbit from a hat, they think it's clever to pluck out a bloody, apparently still beating, human heart. Personally, I prefer a more subtle approach."

Like exploding maggots, I thought!

I was quite relieved when they moved on to look at what seemed a perfectly normal, dark-blue box, the kind of thing you buy in card shops to put a present in if you're too lazy to wrap it.

"What's that?" Rory asked.

"Just something I've been working on for a while," Condini replied.

"But it looks like a perfectly ordinary box," Rory said.

"By now, you should know looks can be deceptive," Condini smiled. "Allow me to demonstrate. Do you have a coin?" Rory handed him a coin which Condini carefully placed in the box. Then, leaving the lid open, he showed us his hand was completely empty. He even rattled the coin about in the box. "Now I close the lid and immediately the coin is gone."

This time, when Condini shook the box, the coin no longer rattled inside.

Rory was enjoying himself. "Go on then," he urged, "bring it back again."

But Condini shook his head. "I did say I was still working on this trick. I'm afraid I can't bring it back."

"But it can't just disappear completely," Rory claimed. "It has to be somewhere."

Condini smiled vaguely. "You are quoting the scientific law, 'Matter can neither be created nor destroyed'. Yes, you are quite right. I'm perfectly certain the coin is somewhere, but if I don't know where, I can hardly bring it back, can I?"

Suddenly I felt very uncomfortable and even Rory didn't seem so sure of himself. "But surely there's no point to the trick if you can't bring the coin back?"

"Isn't there?" Condini gave Rory a very searching look. "I think it might have its uses in particular circumstances. When I have improved the technique, I intend to build a larger version."

"Maybe you could show that at our Christmas Concert?" Rory suggested.

"Oh yes, your concert." Condini looked thoughtfully at Rory. "I only said

I'd think about that."

"But it would be wonderful if you appeared." Rory's eyes shone with excitement. "You'd be the star of the show."

Condini accepted the compliment by inclining his head in a kind of brief bow. "Naturally! But as I said, I am rather out of practice. It is some years since I last appeared in public."

"I'm sure you could do it," Rory gushed.

"Maybe," Condini said. Then he looked at Rory through narrowed eyes. "Perhaps I'd manage better with a little assistance."

Before I could stop him, Rory immediately volunteered. "I'd like to be your assistant."

"So," Condini asked, with a sly smile, "you have ambitions to become the Sorcerer's Apprentice?"

"I'd do exactly what you told me to."

"And swear never to reveal my secrets to a living soul?" Condini insisted.

"I swear!"

Things were moving too quickly for me. I was only too aware that Condini's hold over Rory was increasing, but, before I could say anything, it was Condini who put the brakes on. "I'm still not convinced that it would be wise for me to perform in public again. I shall have to give the matter more serious thought before making my final decision."

"Oh please!" Rory pleaded.

But Condini was unmoved. "It's no

use trying to rush me, but I promise you will have my verdict before the end of the week. Now, come along," he said, shooing us away. "You have taken up enough of my valuable time and I have important matters to attend to."

"Couldn't we stay and help?" Rory pleaded.

"There are some things, my young friend," Condini said sternly, "too deep even for your understanding."

As he ushered us past the shelves, I tried hard to avoid looking at the gruesome contents of the jars. But I was brought to a standstill by one I hadn't noticed before – a single eyeball.

Suspended in the centre of the clear, syrupy liquid it seemed perfectly harmless, and yet somehow the single, bloodshot eye looked deeply concerned. It was almost as if it could see the danger we were in.

Suddenly the eye began to move, swinging shiftily back and forth in the jar, as if it were trying to avoid my stare.

I leapt back in alarm, but Condini said, with a twisted smile, "No need to be afraid, my friend. The eye hasn't come alive! It's only moving because I nudged the shelf with my elbow."

And he put a hand on my shoulder, presumably to comfort me. But far from making me feel better, it made me feel worse. Even through my clothing his hand felt colder than death itself.

## Chapter Seven
### *Hooked*

"ARE YOU COMPLETELY crazy?" I asked
Rory.

We were standing outside the shop
and Rory was under one of the shop
front's red lights. Steam was coming out
of a vent behind his head, making him

look like an angry dragon. "What's bugging you now?"

"You saw the human remains Condini had in there and you heard him saying he ripped them out of people!"

Rory burst out laughing. "You surely didn't believe all those body parts were real?"

"Didn't you?"

Rory shook his head, "No, of course not. They're models he's made to look like the real things."

The swivelling, warning eye had seemed real enough to me!

"And what about the disappearing coin?" I demanded.

"Oh, don't let that fool you," Rory said scornfully. "The box must have a secret compartment, which is where the coin went, and although he hasn't found a way of bringing it back again yet, I'm sure he will."

I said anxiously, "I just wish you hadn't offered to be his assistant for the concert."

"Why not?" Rory asked. "It'll be a great chance to find out how some of his really exciting tricks work."

"That's what's worries me," I said.

But Rory was off into his dream world. "Fancy me getting the chance to work with a real magician! What do you think I'll have to wear? Maybe he's got special costumes for his assistants."

"You ought to ask yourself why he hasn't already got an assistant." I suggested. "Maybe he doesn't have one because they unwillingly donated their organs to

71

his collection!"

"Don't talk wet!" Rory said. "I bet the reason Condini asked me was because he could see I've got a gift for that sort of thing."

"He hasn't even agreed to appear in the concert yet," I said, adding hopefully, "and maybe he won't."

"Oh, I hope he does," Rory said. "Just think, me up on the stage with Condini! What do you suppose Natalie would think about that?"

I got the chance to find out, at school the following day. Rory had rushed off before school started to tell Rolling what Condini had said, when Natalie collared me.

"Brendon, has that crazy friend of yours brought some new and dreadful thing to torment me with today?"

I shook my head. "Not as far as I know."

She sighed with relief. "After what happened yesterday, I seriously considered taking the day off."

"You do realize," I explained, "Rory's only doing it all to impress you."

"Well he needn't bother, if it means scaring me to death with spiders!"

"He didn't mean to scare you, Natalie, in fact he fancies you like mad."

"Fancies me?" Natalie's eyes widened. "I thought he was trying to drive me crazy."

"He's the one who's going crazy," I said, "about wanting to go out with you."

Natalie blushed slightly, but that

didn't stop her saying angrily, "Then why doesn't he just ask me, like any normal human being? Instead of that, he comes on at me with these crazy stunts and makes me look a complete fool in front of everyone."

"He said you'd probably just turn him down if he asked you straight out."

"I probably will now," Natalie said.

"Don't you like Rory?"

Natalie stuck her tongue in her cheek while she thought about him. "I suppose I sort of like him," she reluctantly admitted. "He's got nice hair and he's not bad looking, in a funny sort of way."

"Depending on how you feel about frogs."

Natalie ignored me and thought more about Rory. "He could be quite cute, if only he'd stop behaving like an idiot and scaring me to death."

"You should hear his latest scheme!" I said grimly. "Rory has talked Rolling into letting him ask Condini, the guy who runs the new Joke Shop where Rory gets all his stuff, to do his conjuring in the Christmas Concert. Not only that, but Rory's trying to persuade Condini to let him be his assistant for the show."

"At least Rory might get into less trouble with an adult in control," Natalie suggested.

"You're joking! Condini is the Conjuror from Hell! He's far more dangerous than Rory. Think about it. Where did the flowers come from in the first place? Condini made them and I swear he put the spider in on purpose!"

"He made them?"

"Rory won't believe me, but I've seen horrible things in that shop. I'm positive Condini isn't just a conjuror, he's into real magic."

"You don't mean spells and stuff like that?" Natalie asked, with a slightly nervous giggle. "I don't believe in any of that stuff."

"Nor did I, not until I saw it happening with my own eyes." I told her everything, from the green reptile and the maggots to the human organs.

Natalie screwed up her face. "Sounds disgusting."

"It is," I agreed, "but Condini's got Rory absolutely hooked. He believes everything the old man says and won't listen to me. The trouble is, if Rory doesn't stay away from that place, I think something really terrible's going to happen to him."

Natalie looked concerned. "Like what?"

"I don't know. It's just a feeling I've got. But I'm not joking and only you can stop it."

"Me?"

"I'm sure Rory would listen to you."

Natalie looked doubtful. "I don't want to get mixed up with Rory while he's behaving like a lunatic. After what's happened, Rory's got a bad name and that rubs off on anyone who's seen with him. Until today, when I got the chance to talk to you on your own, I thought you were probably as batty as he is."

"Not really," I said, slumping down

into a walk like the Hunchback of Notre Dame.

"Stop doing that!" she said sharply. "That's exactly the sort of thing I mean!"

"Sorry," I said, suddenly standing bolt upright to attention.

But that didn't satisfy Natalie either. "You just can't stop, can you? You both do everything you can to draw attention to yourselves and I don't want to be around while everyone's staring at you."

She turned and started to walk off, her incredibly white trainers flashing brightly despite the dull day.

"Hey, Natalie, don't go. I promise I'll behave, but you've got to help me stop Rory getting into big trouble with Condini." An idea suddenly struck me. "Look, if you don't want to be seen around school with Rory, why don't you meet us down at the Joke Shop? Then you'd be able to see what Condini's like for yourself."

"I don't know," Natalie said, cautiously.

"You wouldn't want anything dreadful to happen to Rory, would you?"

She sighed. "I suppose not. OK, I'll be there, but there's to be no funny business, right?"

"I promise, and I'll make certain Rory behaves like an angel."

"He better had," Natalie warned menacingly, just as the registration bell rang. "See you at the shop after school. Got to go."

As she ran off, I shouted after her, "Like your new trainers."

Natalie briefly turned, pulled a face,

and then disappeared round the end of
the building.

## Chapter Eight
### *Illusions*

"So where is she?" Rory demanded the minute we arrived at the Joke Shop.

Even the vulture, perched high up on top of the building, seemed to be eagerly scanning the horizon at the prospect of succulent new prey.

After I'd told Rory about my conversation with Natalie, he could hardly contain himself.

"She'll be here," I assured him, hoping she hadn't changed her mind.

"And she did say she thought I was cute, didn't she?" he asked, for the millionth time.

"Yes, I've already told you that!"

"Do you think she meant cute, as in handsome?"

"Ask her yourself!" I growled.

Rory looked hopefully up and down the street. "I would if she was here." When ten minutes had passed and she still hadn't arrived, he turned on me. "This isn't some sort of joke, is it?"

"No, but it would serve you right if it was!" I replied. "It's exactly the kind of stunt you've pulled on other people often enough, including me."

Rory grabbed me by the collar. "You mean, this is a set-up, so you can get your own back?"

"No!" I coughed. "I keep telling you, Natalie said she'd meet us here."

"She'd better," Rory said, shoving me hard against the wall, "or you're for it!"

But we'd both almost given up hope by the time Natalie turned up.

Rory greeted her. "Nice trainers!"

"Don't you start!" she snapped.

"I just said I like them, that's all," Rory said innocently.

"Everybody's been going on at me all day about my trainers," Natalie complained. "I asked Mum for a decent brand, like Nike, or Reebok, but she says they're too dear and gets me these cheap ones which nobody's ever heard of off a market stall. So don't you start as well!"

"I really quite like them," Rory insisted.

"Well, I don't! I'd drop these in a litter bin and walk home barefoot if it wasn't so cold."

"Let's go inside," Rory suggested, "where it's warmer."

Natalie looked warily at the weird shop front.

"You don't have to go in if you don't want to," I said. "We could go for a burger instead."

Rory gave me a sharp look. "You told me Natalie wanted to meet Condini."

Natalie pushed between us. "Stop talking about me as if I'm not here!"

Rory jumped. "Sorry."

"I'll make my own mind up, thank you."

"Of course you will," I agreed. She was a sensible girl. She'd know the right thing to do.

Natalie deliberately kept us both waiting for a few moments before she said, "Let's go in."

I couldn't believe it. "But . . ."

"I want to see for myself," Natalie insisted.

Rory looked suspicious. "See what? What's Bren been telling you?"

Natalie shrugged. "Only that Condini's really weird."

"Rubbish!" Rory snapped, his hand on the door. "He's a perfectly nice old guy."

And sure enough, from the moment Condini set eyes on Natalie, he was!

"My dear young lady, welcome to my humble shop," he simpered. "It's easy to see how my friend came to fall under your spell."

Rory and Natalie blushed like big soft kids as he swept them off on a tour of the shop. Curiously, most of the more repulsive objects were no longer on display.

"Where's the plastic dog turd gone?" I asked.

My reward was another of Condini's pitying looks. "I'm afraid if that's the class of article you require, you'll have to look elsewhere."

Determined not to be put off, I persisted. "There was one in that show-case yesterday."

"True," Condini admitted, "but I've been turning out some of the old stock and we won't be re-ordering that kind of thing any more."

The first chance I got, I whispered to Natalie, "Creepy, isn't he?"

Natalie shook her head. "He's a bit odd, but I think he's quite sweet." Then she sniffed. "Trust you to want a dog turd!"

"I didn't!" I spluttered.

But before I could explain I'd only asked to try and show up Condini, he said, "Young lady, would you like to explore my inner sanctum?"

She smiled. "Oh yes, please."

Condini led us towards the archway, which I couldn't help noticing was no longer green but a delicate pink like the inside of a shell. "Wait until you see all the stuff he keeps in the jars!" I hissed at Natalie.

But the light in the arch wasn't the only change. The skulls had been replaced by harmless-looking dolls and when we reached the jars, the objects floating in them looked more like badly painted plastic replicas than the real things.

Natalie turned on me. "I thought you said these were so life-like they made you feel ill?"

"They were," I said, baffled by the change, "and I did!"

"But even I can see these are just a joke," Natalie continued.

"I'm afraid Brendon has a rather weak stomach," Condini said with a smile. He tapped a jar containing a solid-looking model of the human stomach. "Unlike this one!"

As Natalie and Rory laughed, I said angrily, "These aren't the same ones. They didn't look a bit like this yesterday."

"I'm afraid you were deceived by a trick of the light," Condini said smugly.

Rory cut in. "Why don't you show Natalie your magic box?"

"Ah, yes," Condini smiled. "Since we last met, I have built another version."

Condini reached under the bench and pulled out a much larger, shiny black box. This one was about the size of a portable television and instead of a hinged lid the top parted in the centre and swivelled back like the black wing-cases of some enormous stag beetle.

Rory asked, "Have you managed to solve the problem of getting things back once they've disappeared?"

Condini sighed. "Sadly, no. Whatever goes in, goes for good."

"In that case," Natalie said, bending down, "you're welcome to these!" She dropped her trainers into the box.

Not wanting to be left out, Rory pulled his maths textbook from his bag. "I think I can struggle along without this!" he said, dropping it in the box too.

"You're both crazy!" I said.

"You mean there's nothing you'd like to add to the collection?" Condini asked me. "Nothing you never want to see again?"

I shook my head.

"In that case, gaze upon these items for the last time."

Rory and Natalie bent over the box to make sure their things were still there, before Condini, with a grand flourish, slowly closed the lid. As the two sides slid together, I could have sworn there was a slight hiss, like you hear on the telly in sci-fi stories when the air-lock closes.

Natalie, open-mouthed, eyes sparkling, watched his every move. "Have they gone?"

Condini picked the box up and gave it a shake. "Can you hear anything in there?"

She laughed. "No, but that doesn't mean they've disappeared."

"True, my dear," Condini smiled. "But see for yourselves." He opened the top and tilted the box, to show us that it was completely empty.

"That's amazing," Natalie said.

Rory agreed. "It is, isn't it?"

Condini smiled modestly. "You are both very kind. Just one of my simple illusions, designed to amuse."

Disappointed that Natalie wasn't turning out to be the ally I'd hoped for, I sneered, "Rory told me he doesn't think your trick's all that clever."

"I never!"

"You did! You said the box has got a secret compartment and Condini could easily get the stuff back if he wanted to."

Condini focused the twin beams of his searchlight eyes on me for a few seconds before his face relaxed into a syrupy smile. "Not so!" he said.

Swiftly, he snapped back two clips and the bottom of the box swung open, to show it was only a hollow, empty tube. Then he slid one arm straight through, until his hand waved from the other end. "Think again!"

"That's wonderful!" Natalie cooed.

Condini looked at her very closely before he turned to Rory. "Yesterday you asked me if I would appear in your school concert."

"Yes?"

"I have decided that I will."

"That's fantastic!"

"But with one specific condition."

Rory was so pleased he would have willingly handed over organs from his own body! "Yes, what's that?"

"You wanted to be my assistant, but some of my illusions are very complicated and require two helpers.

I will consent to appear in your concert as long as you and Natalie will both agree to assist me."

"Of course we will," Rory said eagerly, "won't we?"

"I'd love to," Natalie beamed.

"It will mean a good deal of hard work and rehearsal together between now and the night of the concert," Condini warned.

"That should be fun," Natalie said, with a sideways glance at Rory.

Rory grinned back at her, looking like an ape being offered a bunch of bananas. "Too right!"

Then Natalie gave me a brief moment of hope, as a look of doubt crossed her face. "But I'm not sure I've got anything I could wear for a magic show."

"But I have," Condini smirked, handing her a tiny package, about the size of a matchbox. "What's in there should be exactly your size."

"In here?" Natalie laughed. "You couldn't possibly get a dress to fit me into something as small as this!"

"Open it up and see for yourself," Condini urged.

She did and a tiny slip of material appeared. She pulled the loose end and metres of gossamer material followed. It was like a conjuror producing coloured bunting from nowhere, but much more impressive.

The cloth was midnight blue, dotted with tiny silver stars and moons, and was so light that it practically floated in the air.

"I've never seen anything so beauti-ful," Natalie whispered.

I knew then, I'd lost! And, when Condini looked towards me, there was no doubting the look of total triumph in his evil eyes. Any hope I had that Natalie might help me rescue Rory from the old man's clutches had disappeared along with her trainers.

## Chapter Nine
# *The Concert*

A COUPLE OF days before the concert,
Rory said, "You should see the latest
thing Condini's made for the show."

It was almost the first thing he'd said
to me for ages. Without much interest I
asked, "So what is it?"

"Oh, I can't tell you," Rory replied. "I'm sworn to secrecy, but you ought to see it."

"Why mention it," I grumbled, "if you can't talk about it?"

"Sorry. Bren, have you decided what you're doing for the concert?"

"Nothing. If I have my way, I'll be stopping at home that night. See you," I mumbled and wandered off to see if I could find anyone else to talk to, preferably someone not involved with the concert. That wasn't easy. Rolling had roped in almost everyone.

But if I'm honest, what really made me want to keep as far away as possible from the concert was pure jealousy. Since the evening we'd met Natalie at the Joke Shop, Rory called for Natalie every morning instead of me. At school they were hardly ever apart and they spent all their free time, including weekends, rehearsing with Condini. Rory had even started combing his hair and cleaning his trainers.

On the actual day of the concert, just when I thought I'd succeeded in avoiding it altogether, Rolling suddenly said, "Brendon, I want you to help out backstage."

I tried to protest, "Mrs Stone, I . . ."

But she wasn't listening. "As you're one of the few people not appearing, Brendon, you can help Mr Paget with the lights and curtains. I'll tell him to expect you straight after school."

Mr Paget takes us for Information Technology, so naturally I spent the first hour showing him how to use the computer which controls the stage lighting, so that people wouldn't have to perform in total darkness.

Condini turned up an hour before curtain up and stowed all his stuff away in a room to which only he had the key.

I offered to carry stuff for him, but he waved me aside. "No, thank you, Brendon. I have my own band of willing helpers," he said. And when I saw Rory and Natalie struggling with a large wickerwork hamper, I was happy to leave them to it.

When the concert finally got underway, it wasn't so bad. Mr Paget only plunged the stage into darkness a couple of times and, as one of those unexpected blackouts cut short Mrs Greenhalgh's caterwauling through a selection from *Annie Get Your Gun*, nobody seemed to mind.

Rolling ran backwards and forwards, getting in everyone's way. She was delighted the hall was packed to capacity, which meant the school fund would receive a great deal of money.

Of course, apart from wanting to see their own 'little darlings' do their bit, most people had come because Condini was top of the bill, and midway through the second half they started getting a bit restless. While Snotty Hawkins, the last item on the programme before Condini, squeaked through his flute solo, slow handclapping broke out.

I was watching Snotty from the wings, when Rory and Natalie brushed by me.

Reluctantly, I had to admit that Natalie looked fantastic in the blue dress, and Rory, who wore a long flowing cloak made from similar material, looked OK too.

"Hi!" I said, but although Rory looked at me, his eyes stared straight through me. His face was completely blank and he didn't speak. "Are you OK?" I asked, but when he still didn't reply, I turned to Natalie. "What's up with Rory?"

But she didn't answer either. They both stared straight ahead with the same empty expression.

At first I thought they were simply very nervous about working with Condini, but as they stood together, silent and completely still, I couldn't help wondering if it was something far more sinister. They behaved as if they were in some sort of deep trance.

Thankfully, a few minutes later, Snotty choked and we were able to close the curtains. While Rolling went out in front to thank everyone, Natalie and Rory glided into action backstage, setting up their apparatus under Condini's directions. One piece, totally shrouded in black material, was so large that, despite it being on wheels, it took all three of them to get it on stage.

I realized that whilst Rolling was almost finished and about to announce the star act, the apparatus wasn't ready. To help out, I grabbed their last piece of equipment, but Condini rushed over and snatched it from me. "Leave that!" he snapped.

"Sorry ! Only trying to help."

Furious, Condini thrust his face close to mine and snarled, "All I want is for you to mind your own business and stay as far away from me as possible."

As I reeled back from the hideous stench of Condini's breath and the sheer ferocity of his attack, Mrs Stone proudly announced, "And now, let's all settle back and prepare to be astonished by the amazing talents of Condini."

Thunderous applause burst out as Condini, his face suddenly wreathed in smiles, stepped out into the spotlight.

But, as his two obedient assistants followed him on to the stage, I couldn't help wondering if this was the moment I'd been dreading ever since Rory had first entered the Joke Shop?

## Chapter Ten
# *The Disappearing Act*

A GOLDEN BALL, lit from inside, was floating at about waist height in front of Condini. He looked as if he was controlling it with his hands and as they moved left, so did the ball. It was an old trick and we all thought we knew it was supported by some kind of invisible wire.

But Condini surprised us all by suddenly sending the ball hurtling out into the auditorium like a brilliant meteor. For a few moments the glowing ball hung in the darkness above the audience before it swooped back, barely skimming their heads.

His next trick was another old one, sawing a girl in half, Natalie being the girl. As always, she lay down in the wooden box so that, when the lid was shut, her feet poked out of one end and her silver-blonde hair hung down from her head at the other.

But Condini didn't use a saw to cut through the box. He didn't touch it at all. He stood well back and pointed to the centre of the side of the box, where he wanted to start the cut. Slowly, a pin-point of glowing red appeared. The red glow quickly became white heat and as he moved his finger down there was a faint smell of charred wood.

"Where's he got that thing plugged in?" Mr Paget demanded, looking at his control panel.

"What thing?" I asked.

"Well, he must be using some sort of laser," Mr Paget said, scratching his head.

"I don't think so," I replied quietly. "Not Condini!"

Condini had moved to the other side and was repeating the process. Throughout, Natalie smiled at the audience and waggled her feet. When he had cut right through the box, Condini inserted two metal dividers and then swung the two halves of Natalie and the box apart. During the tumultuous applause Condini put the box back together and Natalie stepped out, completely unharmed.

But fascinating as his tricks were, I was far more interested in Condini's assistants. Not only did they appear to know exactly what to do, but they even managed to anticipate things going wrong.

While Condini was performing a trick with three coloured balls Rory, for no apparent reason, took a sudden step to his right. Seconds later, Condini dropped a ball which bounced across the stage, straight into Rory's waiting hands. Had he not moved, the ball would have run off into the wings and the trick been spoilt. But how could he possibly have known that was going to happen?

They both behaved as if they shared the same mind. No longer able to think for themselves, but completely hooked in to Condini's brain. Not that anybody else seemed to notice anything odd about their behaviour.

Condini was introducing the last trick and I have to admit I was relieved that my suspicion that something awful was going to happen had turned out to be unfounded.

I watched happily as the old man walked up towards the large object at the back of the stage, but when he whisked the black cloth off my heart skipped a beat. I suddenly realized this was a man-sized version of the box he'd used to make Natalie's trainers disappear – the one from which he'd never managed to get anything back.

The box being on wheels, it was possible to see right underneath the whole thing. Condini walked up a flight of steps to open the door in the black front panel and show it was absolutely empty. Then he twirled the box round, opened another door and revealed Natalie standing behind it.

Condini closed one door and turned that side to the back before he announced, "I will now amaze you all by making my special friend and assistant, Rory, completely disappear."

I went cold. All my fears were true after all. This was what Condini had been leading up to all these weeks!

"Rory," Condini instructed, "step into the box."

Under my breath I pleaded with Rory, "No, don't do it!"

Mr Paget, who was standing right next to me, said, "Brendon, don't be silly, it's only another trick."

I said grimly, "No, it isn't. If Rory gets into that box he'll never be seen again!"

Mr Paget laughed at first, but when he saw the deadly serious expression on my face he looked baffled. "But that wouldn't be any sort of trick. Besides, it's impossible. You can't *really* make things disappear into thin air."

"Condini can, I've seen him do it – and so has Rory. He knows how dangerous this is!"

But when I looked back at the stage, Rory, still in his trance-like state, was already walking up a flight of steps towards the box's open door.

"I must stop him," I shouted.

"Hey, wait . . ." Mr Paget said.

Dodging his outstretched hand, I ran on to the stage. As I appeared, the puzzled murmur from the audience made Condini turn round. "Stay back," he warned me. "There's nothing you can do now."

From her front row seat, Rolling shouted, "Brendon, you're spoiling everything. Leave the stage immediately! Mr Paget, stop him."

Condini, his face purple with rage, yelled, "Leave him to me!" He pointed his bony finger at me, just as he had while sawing through the cabinet. Instantly, through my clothing I felt a warm glow. But I wasn't a cabinet, I could move, and before the heat increased I dodged out of the way.

"You can't save Rory now," Condini screamed, "he's mine!"

"Not yet he isn't," I replied. Running up the steps after Rory, I tried to grab hold of him, but I only succeeded in stepping on the train of his flowing cloak. There was a rending sound from the material, the cloak floated off Rory's back and suddenly he was standing at the top of the steps, looking totally baffled.

"What's happening?" Rory mumbled, rubbing his eyes as if he'd just woken from a deep sleep.

"You are going in that box!" Condini

shouted. "That's what's happening."

And with that, Condini made a desperate rush up the steps and lunged at Rory. But, as he rushed past me, I pushed Rory off the steps and then gave the old man a helpful shove straight through the open door and into the box.

"No!" Condini roared. "Natalie, help me!"

But by the time Natalie came round the front, I'd slammed the door. For a second there was complete silence, then uproar broke out. Above it, I heard several voices.

Rory kept asking, "What's going on, Bren?"

Rolling was shouting, "Brendon, my office, NOW!"

And Mr Paget grabbed hold of me and

demanded, "What on earth do you think you were doing, boy?"

"I'll show you," I said, reaching for the door, intending to reveal what had happened to Condini. But I never got the chance. As I reached out to grab the door handle, the box burst into flames.

The blaze quickly spread to the surrounding curtains and people screamed as they headed for the emergency exits. Rory and I were making for the nearest door, when we realized Natalie hadn't moved. Above her head light bulbs exploded in the heat, sending down showers of broken glass around her, but Natalie stood motionless, calmly awaiting Condini's next instruction.

Rory ran back and tugged at her arm, crying, "Natalie! You must get out of here." But she completely ignored him. "What's wrong with her?" he shouted.

I suddenly knew. "It's the dress."

Rory stared at me as if I'd gone off my head. "What's that got to do with anything?"

"Don't you see? You were in Condini's power until I accidentally ripped off your cloak," I explained, "and so is Natalie while she's still wearing the dress he gave her. Come on, we'll have to carry her out!"

## Chapter Eleven
### The Phoenix

THAT NIGHT, OUR school wasn't the only place needing fire engines. Once we'd got Natalie sorted out and were on our way home, we passed the Joke Shop to discover that it too had become a flaming inferno.

"Just look at that!" Rory gasped.

The whole place was ablaze. The fire was far too intense for the firemen to do anything about it, but they still wore breathing apparatus to keep out the sulphurous stench of the thick yellowy-green smoke which was billowing in waves from the building.

We watched in silence. But when I looked up to the roof, I saw the feathers on the vulture's outstretched wings had caught light. "Hey, look up there!" I cried.

The bird's fixing must have been destroyed, for suddenly the flaming bird launched itself into the air. We thought it would crash to the ground, but it didn't. Instead, leaving a trail of sparks behind it, it soared off across the night sky, until it was totally consumed by its own flames.

"Wow!" Natalie whispered in disbelief.

"I just hope it really *is* a vulture and not a phoenix," I said quietly.

"What's a phoenix?" Rory asked.

"The mythical bird which was supposed to rise again from its own ashes," Natalie explained.

In spite of the fire's intense heat, we all three shivered before we finally set off together.

One year later:

# SNAKES ALIVE!

Yesterday police called a snake-handler to the premises of the High Street dress shop, Modern Modes, when a poisonous snake was discovered in one of the changing rooms being used by teenager Natalie Gibson.

Captured with difficulty, the reptile was identified by the handler as a highly dangerous Tiger Snake. "One of the most venomous varieties known to man and normally found only in Australia."

Modern Modes opened only recently on the site of Condini's Joke Shop, which burned down in mysterious circumstances last year after the owner disappeared.

"We don't know how the creature got in there, as the shop door doesn't even have a letter box," a police spokeswoman said, "and we are treating the incident as extremely serious. Whoever released the snake must have known how deadly it was."

# READ MORE IN PUFFIN

For children of all ages, Puffin represents quality and variety – the very best in publishing today around the world.

For complete information about books available from Puffin – and Penguin – and how to order them, contact us at the appropriate address below. Please note that for copyright reasons the selection of books varies from country to country.

**On the worldwide web**: www.puffin.co.uk

**In the United Kingdom**: Please write to *Dept. EP, Penguin Books Ltd, Bath Road, Harmondsworth, West Drayton, Middlesex UB7 ODA*

**In the United States**: Please write to *Consumer Sales, Penguin USA, P.O. Box 999, Dept. 17109, Bergenfield, New Jersey 07621-0120*. VISA and MasterCard holders call 1-800-253-6476 to order Penguin titles

**In Canada**: Please write to *Penguin Books Canada Ltd, 10 Alcorn Avenue, Suite 300, Toronto, Ontario M4V 3B2*

**In Australia**: Please write to *Penguin Books Australia Ltd, P.O. Box 257, Ringwood, Victoria 3134*

**In New Zealand**: Please write to *Penguin Books (NZ) Ltd, Private Bag 102902, North Shore Mail Centre, Auckland 10*

**In India**: Please write to *Penguin Books India Pvt Ltd, 706 Eros Apartments, 56 Nehru Place, New Delhi 110 019*

**In the Netherlands**: Please write to *Penguin Books Netherlands bv, Postbus 3507, NL-1001 AH Amsterdam*

**In Germany**: Please write to *Penguin Books Deutschland GmbH, Metzlerstrasse 26, 60594 Frankfurt am Main*

**In Spain**: Please write to *Penguin Books S. A., Bravo Murillo 19, 1° B, 28015 Madrid*

**In Italy**: Please write to *Penguin Italia s.r.l., Via Felice Casati 20, I–20124 Milano.*

**In France**: Please write to *Penguin France S. A., 17 rue Lejeune, F–31000 Toulouse*

**In Japan**: Please write to *Penguin Books Japan, Ishikiribashi Building, 2–5–4, Suido, Bunkyo-ku, Tokyo 112*

**In South Africa**: Please write to *Longman Penguin Southern Africa (Pty) Ltd, Private Bag X08, Bertsham 2013*